*Best wishes for your version of the journey!*

*Ian Thorp.*

# THE

# GREAT YEAR

Understanding 2012 and Beyond

*by*

# IAN THORP

*with illustrations by*

# THE AUTHOR

ARCHIVE
publishing

## ACKNOWLEDGEMENTS

I would like to acknowledge, with gratitude: those from past and present generations whose pioneering work inspired me to write; those who have materially contributed to this book, and those whose support and interest kept this project alive when my 'inner saboteur' appeared to have the upper hand.

Particular thanks to the many fellow travellers who read, proofed and gave critical feedback of the manuscript: Dr. Marie Angelo, Anne Baring, Susannah Brown, Mike Edwards QHP, Alison Gaffney, Celia Gunn, Hazel Marshall, Josephine Sellers, Dr. Anthony Thorley, and especially my partner Jacqueline May.

First Published in Great Britain in 2011 by Archive Publishing.

Text © 2011, Ian Thorp
Illustrations © 2011 Ian Thorp

Ian Thorp asserts the moral right to be identified as the author of this work

A CIP Record for this book is available from The British Cataloguing-in-Publication data office

ISBN 978 1 906289 13 3  (Printed paper case)

Printed and bound in Latvia
by Dardedze Holography

www.archivepublishing.co.uk

www.transpersonalbooks.com

A NOTE ON

# *The Great Year: Understanding 2012 and Beyond*

This story was inspired by all the speculation and discussion surrounding the significance of 2012 and in particular the Winter Solstice. The central theme is to remind the reader of the planet we live on in relation to the rest of our solar system - the need to reawaken knowledge and thereby the heart, so that the future is seen as positive and affirming - both relevant and vital in these times.

Ian Thorp's engaging narrative and imaginative paintings combine in a story that shows each of us, adults and children alike, how we can change our lives and the fate of the Earth for the better, through the choices we make.

Our story begins with a child from Earth finding himself aboard the 'ship' of a visiting time-traveller from across the Cosmos. The 'Captain', before explaining the purpose of their journey to his officers and crew, helps Jack to understand more about the history of his wonderful planet and her place in the Cosmos. The young crew enter into the spirit of their journey as they begin to realise the full significance of what is happening to Earth, the beautiful planet in front of them, and how through the re-telling of the story, at what is seen as a crucial time of development for the planet, they may inform the inhabitants of the choices they have for their future well-being. Eventually a solution is found to bring to their attention the changes that are already taking place, and to help prepare them for those that must surely happen, for them to restore their collective and individual soul.

## IAN THORP

Ian Thorp is an artist, writer, singer and musician. He has been involved in the design, print and publishing trade for most of his life and currently runs transpersonalbooks.com and Archive Publishing where he publishes the work of Anne Baring, Ian Gordon-Brown, Barabara Somers and many others. Part of his vision and that of transpersonalbooks.com is to bring into the public domain transformative material for the benefit of the individual. It is envisioned that through the expansion of consciousness soul may be repatriated at all levels and the true balance of life and harmony restored.

Ian is a practising Psychotherapist with an MA in Transpersonal Arts and Practice. Currently he is preparing a series of books for children, to help them prepare for the challenges that are facing all of us at this crucial time of choice.

He has three grown-up children and a granddaughter from his first marriage and now lives in Dorset with his partner, two cats and an allotment.

# THE BEAUTIFUL PLANET

Jack found himself on the deck of a large sailing ship, not one that he had ever seen before. It was awesome, with huge masts and sails, lots of rigging and ropes. It all felt good and so real, with a firm wooden deck under his feet and lots of people busily adjusting the sails and performing other tasks.

Jack was startled, as a foreign figure in a bright, lavish uniform, whom he presumed to be the Captain, gave an order to 'heave-to'. Jack didn't know what this meant but as the ship began slowing down he presumed it must have something to do with that.

'Wow!' he exclaimed, as he suddenly realised he had understood what the Captain had said. Worried that they might have heard him, he looked around, but they were busy studying something shown on a large vista screen on the poop deck. Again he was suprised to see such technology on an old-fashioned sailing ship. Jack moved closer to see what they were watching. To his surprise the Captain turned to him and said,

'Welcome aboard, Jack, we've been expecting you for sometime. I hope you will not be too confused by the way we speak, but as I was just explaining to the Midshipmen here, the language of navigating the cosmos has not changed for centuries.' Jack recalled the word 'midshipmen' from a deep memory, as meaning naval trainees. The Captain continued, 'The terminology started and still prevails on board ships, boats and aeroplanes that navigate and sail the seas and airways of the beautiful-looking planet below us.' On hearing that, a shudder ran through Jack's body. He broke into a cold sweat as he ran to the side of the ship. 'I'd better explain this to all the young crew members,' continued the Captain, 'I doubt if any of them have been to this part of the Cosmos before, let alone to Earth herself.' Jack could not believe what was happening to him; they were floating in space and he was looking down at his own… planet!

As if he knew what Jack was feeling, the Captain spoke to him reassuringly.

'Jack, we know of your interest in your home planet. We also know that you spend time worrying about what's happening on Earth. So as we are in this part of the Cosmos for a reason we thought it might be helpful for you to join us and find some of the answers for yourself.' He called the three Midshipmen over to where he was standing. 'These are my most junior officers, all about your age, and all here to discover the wonders of the Cosmos and in particular Earth, so you will be of great help to them as you live on Earth. This is Ylime the senior Midshipman, Mas next and this is Eticilef.'

'Strange names,' Jack thought, as they greeted him.

The Captain, who in some way reminded Jack of his Grandfather, spoke again.

'I loved to listen to the many stories of this magical planet read to me as a child. They inspired me to read more about the Ancient history of Earth as I grew up. That interest has continued throughout my adult life, especially after visiting Earth a few hundred years ago.' Jack's mind started to reel. 'I have read and studied the myths, legends and philosophies, all of which are now stored in the archives of the Library on board this ship. I realise it's not always easy for you to answer the many questions in your head and so I hope that, by travelling with us, you and the Midshipmen here will all benefit from first-hand experience.'

Speechless and spellbound, Jack was hardly able to concentrate on what was being said. He was trying desperately to get a grasp on what was happening to him.

'Have you visited any Ancient sites in your country, Jack?'

'Yes,' he blurted out, 'My parents, sisters and I went to a place called Stonehenge, a lot of huge tall stones built in a sort of circle, but I didn't really understand it.'

'Would you like to hear how it relates to what you see around you up here?'

'Yes, please!' Jack answered, excited at the prospect, especially as he had some new friends to share in the adventure.

Stonehenge, Wiltshire, England - circa 3000 BCE

Kerbstone 52, Newgrange, Ireland - circa 3200 BCE - where the Sun penetrates deep into the central chamber at dawn on the Winter solstice.

# OBSERVERS AND RECORDERS

'For thousands of years,' the Captain continued, 'the inhabitants of Earth had lived a life in harmony with nature and the Cosmos that surrounded them. Through long and careful observation, they had watched the Sun, Moon and other celestial bodies moving in patterns against the backdrop of the fixed stars; these all being viewable with the naked eye from Earth. Wanting to learn more, the inhabitants of Earth at that time had set up single tall stones to observe the shadow that was cast by the Sun's rays by day and the Moon's beams by night. Later they built alignments or circles of stones that allowed for more accurate observation and where ritual and ceremony could take place. There are still many fine examples of these scattered across the different continents of the planet below and the one Jack has just mentioned is one of the more famous.' Jack could imagine people weaving amongst the stones in long ceremonial robes.

'Later, as understanding increased about the cycles of the planets, so the stone alignments became more elaborate, some becoming enclosed constructions or 'cairns', later known as 'star temples', where the rays of the Sun or Moon shining through an opening could light up or illumine the passage deep into the cairn. These temples all helped the Ancient astronomers to understand and mark the cycles of the 'wanderers', the Sun, Moon and planets, as they appeared to move around the sky in the evening, night and early morning; indeed many of the cairns carried intricate carvings in the stones to record the passage of the planets in question.'

'When I visited Newgrange in Ireland with my Grandparents,' Jack told them, 'Grandma said the markings were called 'rock art'. Now, from what you are saying, I guess what I was seeing were the notes made by the astronomers. It's as if the stones are carrying the encoded ancient knowledge of their observations.'

# THE SUN

'That's right, Jack,' the Captain said, 'and unlike your ancestors who made the carvings, you, like many other people on Earth nowadays, take the Sun for granted. Thousands of years ago, some inhabitants of Earth worshipped the Sun, believing it to be a god with great influence over them. They knew that without its influence their lives would not be possible. In the country known as Egypt, for a time, they changed their whole belief system which was previously polytheistic, meaning many gods, to monotheistic, or one god, to whom they gave the name Aten, the Sun god.

Likewise, in Ancient Greece there was a theory that the Sun was at the centre of the Cosmos with everything else revolving around it including the Earth, Moon and other planets.' Then Jack laughed in astonishment as the Captain said, 'At yet another time in their development, many inhabitants thought the surface of the planet to be flat; that if you sailed too far in a ship you would end up falling over the edge into outer darkness.' Jack could immediately see how silly this idea seemed especially from his new vantage point out in space, as the shape of Earth as well as the other planets could be clearly seen from here.

The Captain continued, 'With the passing of the years, the naked-eye view gave way to a belief, based on calculations, that Earth was neither animate nor anything more than a spherical planet orbiting the Sun. The sense of awe and wonder people felt for 'her' began to fade, and they began to speak of Earth as 'it', an inanimate object. Likewise the name Cosmos, meaning harmonious system, was changed to Universe.

As you know, the Sun really does influence life on Earth; too much Sun and vegetation and crops burn up and die, human skin dries and ages, animals die from the drought. Too little, and plants might not even start to grow; a delicate balance.'

## Phases of the Moon

The Last Quarter

The Waning Crescent

The Waning Gibbous

SUN

The New Moon

Earth

The Full Moon

The Waxing Crescent

The Waxing Gibbous

The First Quarter

# The Moon

As the ship came closer to the Moon, Jack realised it was a huge sphere and asked, 'Why doesn't it always look like that from my home?'

'The Moon is the nearest of the seven wandering stars to Earth,' answered Ylime, 'And past inhabitants had always been intrigued by the way the Moon appeared to change shape.' He flashed an image on the virtual screen as he explained. 'The cycle begins with an invisible new Moon, when the Moon is between the Sun and the Earth and you can only see it as a faint shadow. It continues through various stages of waxing, or looking bigger, as more sunlight is able to shine on it, to full Moon, when the Earth is between the Sun and the Moon. Then the Moon appears to grow smaller, as she turns to waning back to invisibility before starting a new 27 day and 8 hour cycle.'

Mas reminded Jack, 'The Moon's and the Earth's cycles are synchronous so you only see one side from Earth. Also from the Moon, Earth got the name for moonth or month and as you know, you have twelve of these in a Year. The Moon's cycle does not fit with that of the Sun so it must seem strange, to you on Earth, to have a Moon that sometimes appears at night and sometimes during the day depending on the phase of her cycle. Before the telescope was invented some cultures lived a thirteen month year to make it more harmonious as there are often thirteen Full Moons in your year. It's so much easier for us, as observers from out in space, to see how all this happens.'

Jack was even more impressed as Ylime told him 'The Moon's cycle is extremely powerful, as the influence of her gravitational pull governs the ebb and flow of all the tides in the seas, oceans and waters across the face of the planet below, as well as the procreative cycle within the women of Earth.' Jack made a mental note to look up 'procreative' in the dictionary to see what it meant.

# NIGHT AND DAY

Jack asked, 'Can we see how night and day happens from up here?' Mas beckoned him across the deck to listen to the tall Lieutenant who was starting to explain.

'The Earth revolves on its axis whilst also orbiting the Sun.' Seeing the blank looks on the faces of Jack and his friends, the Lieutenant remembered the difficulty he once had in grasping this when he was their age and so he suggested, 'You might find it easier to imagine a line like a large bar going through the Earth from the North Pole, which you can see from the ship, through to the South Pole, around which the Earth might spin or rotate.'

'But I have never felt the Earth move at home.' Jack interjected.

'That's because a force called gravity holds you firmly in place - otherwise you might fly off into space!' joked Mas.

The Lieutenant put a mind map on the virtual screen as he explained, 'The Earth's axis is tilted from the perpendicular by 23.45° to the plane it makes as it orbits around the Sun. So the Earth does not present an upright face to the Sun, it is always at an angle.' (see his image on the next page)

With this image in their minds, they were then able to see how, as Earth rotates on its axis, one side of the planet would be turned towards the Sun and so in daylight, whilst the other would be turned away and in night time or darkness. As the rotation continued, so daylight would progress across the surface of the Earth facing the Sun, leaving the area that was turning to face away from the Sun in darkness. So the phenomenon of night and day was explained and understood, especially by Jack as he could now see it happening with his own eyes.

The Lieutenant decided to be bold and put another image on the virtual screen.

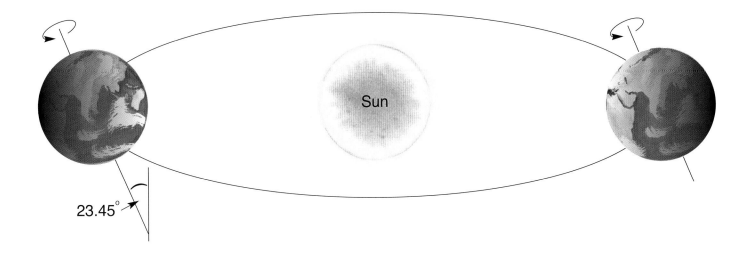

Night and Day

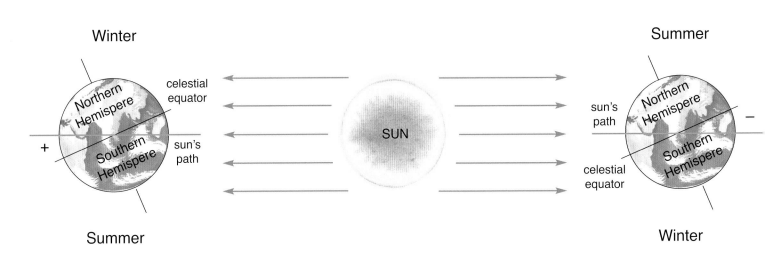

Winter

Summer

Northern Hemispere

celestial equator

sun's path

Southern Hemispere

+

SUN

sun's path

Northern Hemispere

−

celestial equator

Southern Hemispere

Summer

Winter

The Seasons

# THE SEASONS

'It is this tilting that gives Earth its four seasons of the year. What are their names, Jack?' asked the Lieutenant.

'Spring, Summer, Autumn and Winter,' Jack replied.

'Since the axis is tilted,' the Lieutenant continued, 'different parts of the planet are facing the Sun at different times of the year and this affects the amount of sunlight each receives. Summer is warmer than winter in each hemisphere because the Sun's rays hit the Earth at a more direct angle, making the days longer than the nights. During the winter, the Sun's rays hit the Earth at an extreme angle and the days become short and colder in comparison. The two poles get no Sun at all in their respective midwinters.'

The Lieutenant continued, 'There are four main points in this cycle. The first two are called the Solstices, which are the days when the Sun's path, represented by the orange line, reaches its farthest point north or south - called the degree of declination - from the celestial equator, the black line on the diagram. The winter solstice occurs on December 21st or 22nd and marks the beginning of winter; this is the shortest day of the year. The summer solstice occurs on June 21st and marks the beginning of summer; this is the longest day of the year. The reverse for the Southern Hemisphere.'

'My birthday is two days later,' whispered Jack to Mas.

'The second two are the Equinoxes, when day and night are of equal length. They occur when the Sun crosses the celestial equator, the orange line crossing the black line on the diagram. The vernal or spring equinox occurs on March 20th or 21st in the Northern Hemisphere; the beginning of autumn (fall) in the Southern Hemisphere. The autumnal equinox occurs on September 22nd or 23rd in the Northern Hemisphere; the beginning of spring in the Southern Hemisphere.'

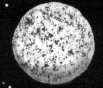

Sun

Mars

Mercury

Uranus

Saturn

Moon

Neptune

Jupiter

Venus

Earth or 'Gaia'

# THE SEVEN WANDERING STARS

'Several times I have heard the word 'wanderers' and 'wandering stars' being used. What are they? Can someone explain, please?' asked Jack.

The Captain told him about the ancient tradition. 'From their observations, your ancestors on Earth named the stars that didn't move 'the fixed stars' and those that did the 'Seven wandering stars'. Working outwards from the Earth, there was the Moon, Mercury, Venus, Sun, Mars, Jupiter and farthest out, Saturn, all of which could be seen from Earth with the naked eye as they travelled around the Cosmos; observed and recorded by your ancestors long before the telescope was invented. The ancient people knew the duration of these cycles in relation to Earth and the fixed stars that they appeared to pass in front of as they revolved around her.

Later it was accepted that the Sun was, in fact, the star at the centre of this solar system and that Earth was a planet orbiting around it, with the Moon orbiting the Earth. This calculated construct has become useful for operating technological systems, but,' - he looked Jack in the eye - 'your embodied experience is what really matters, and that is that you still observe the Sun rise each morning and set below the horizon each evening. As you do not feel the motion of the Earth, it still appears to you as if the Sun and planets move round her?' Jack nodded in agreement. 'Quite different and yet equally acceptable viewpoints,' added the Captain as he explained that the picture was not to scale, nor in proportion, as in reality the planets could not be viewed in one small area as on the pages of a book. 'With the aid of the telescope, two further planets were discovered orbiting the Sun. They were given the names Uranus and Neptune and you can see them better in the next picture which shows more accurately the relative sizes and positions of the planets in their order outwards from the Sun.' (over page)

Sun — the star at the centre of this Solar system. It appears, as viewed from Earth, to take 365 days, or one Earth year, to pass in front of all twelve of the constellations. It is 9.7 times the diameter of Jupiter and 109 times the diameter of Earth.

Mercury — 3 months (87.97 Earth days) to orbit the Sun as it passes through all twelve constellations.
57.9 million km from the Sun – 0.33 times the diameter of Earth.

Venus — 9 months (224.7 Earth days) to orbit the Sun as it passes through all twelve constellations.
108.2 million km from the Sun – 0.95 times the diameter of Earth.

Earth — 1 Year (365.26 Earth days) to orbit the Sun. The Earth rotates on its own axis every 23 hours and 56 minutes or one Earth Day – one moon.
149.6 million km from the Sun.

Mars — 2 years (687 Earth days) to orbit the Sun as it passes through all twelve constellations (spending approx. two months in each) – two tiny moons.
227.9 million km from the Sun – 0.53 times the diameter of Earth.

Jupiter — 12 Earth years (4337 Earth days) to orbit the Sun (spending a full year travelling in each constellation) Jupiter has 4 large moons, 16 in total.
778.3 million km from the Sun – 11.2 times the diameter of Earth – the largest planet in this Solar system.

Saturn — 29.5 Earth years (10760 days) to orbit the Sun (spending approximately two years in each constellation) Saturn has more than 33 moons.
1427 million km from the Sun – 9.4 times the diameter of Earth – the second largest planet in this Solar system.

Uranus — 84.07 Earth years (30700 days) for Uranus to orbit the Sun (spending approx. seven years in each constellation) Uranus has 5 large moons.
2871 million km from the Sun – 4 times the diameter of Earth – the third largest planet in this Solar system.

Neptune — 165 Earth years (60200 days) for Neptune to orbit the Sun (spending approximately fourteen years in each constellation)
4497 million km from the Sun – 3.8 times the diameter of Earth – the fourth largest planet in this Solar system.

# THE DAYS OF THE WEEK

As daylight started to creep across the planet below, the tall Lieutenant pointed it out to Jack. 'The people on Earth will soon be waking up to Saturn's day, the day of the planet Saturn, part of the week-end as you call it on Earth.' He then asked Jack to tell the Midshipmen the names of the other days which Jack did readily. 'Now,' the Lieutenant continued, 'can any of you remember where the names of the days of the week might have come from?' Jack had an urge to answer and yet didn't know whether what he wanted to say made sense, so he blurted out, 'From the Seven wandering stars?'

'That was an inspired guess, Jack,' said the Lieutenant, and to the others, 'please write them all down and add the French and Latin names for good measure so you can see the similarities across different languages.'

| PLANET | FRENCH | ENGLISH | LATIN | DAY |
|--------|--------|---------|-------|-----|
| Sun | Dimanche | Sunday | dies Solis | (day of Sun) |
| Moon | Lundi | Monday | dies Lunae | (day of Moon) |
| Mars | Mardi | Tuesday | dies Martis | (day of Mars) |
| Mercury | Mercredi | Wednesday | dies Mercurii | (day of Mercury) |
| Jupiter | Jeudi | Thursday | dies Jovis | (day of Jupiter) |
| Venus | Vendredi | Friday | dies Veneris | (day of Venus) |
| Saturn | Samedi | Saturday | dies Saturni | (day of Saturn) |

Eticilef, the youngest Midshipman, asked, 'Can someone explain why some of the English days sound so different from the French and Latin?'

The Lieutenant explained, 'It's because some of the English names were changed to those of Nordic gods, such as Thor on Thursday and Freya on Friday, as a result of invasions of Britain by Scandinavian peoples a long time ago.'

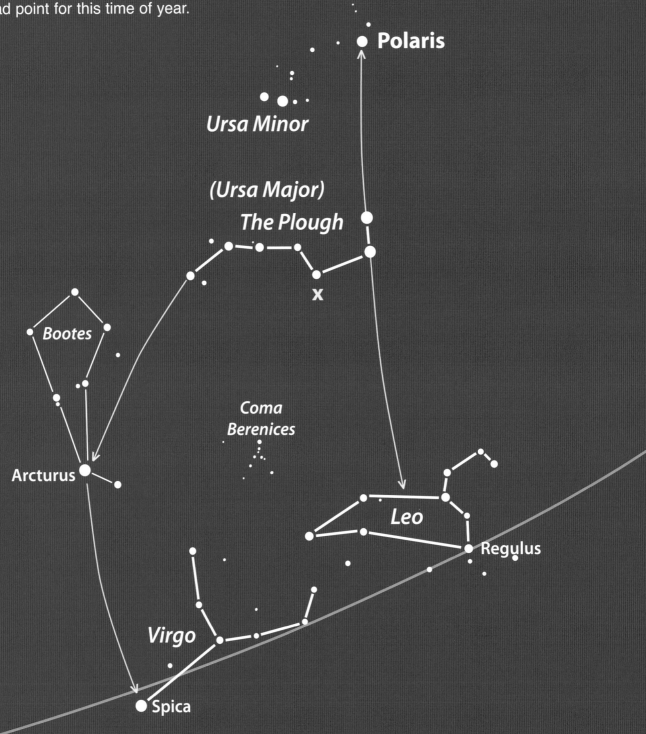

Spring in the Northern Hemisphere:
The Plough is probably one of the
best known constellations and a
useful sign post to others, especially
those of the Zodiac on the ecliptic.
The x marks the approximate overhead point for this time of year.

*Cassiopeia*

*Polaris*

*Ursa Minor*

*(Ursa Major)*
*The Plough*

x

*Bootes*

*Coma*
*Berenices*

Arcturus

*Leo*

Regulus

*Virgo*

Spica

*Corvus*

# DIFFICULTY SEEING THE STARS

The Captain, who was in a jovial mood, recounted. 'I remember I had difficulty as a young Midshipman, trying to understand how all these things would seem from the perspective of Earth; so much easier, I thought at the time, to be born on Earth and grow up seeing it all as a matter of course from your own garden or bedroom window.' He stopped abruptly as he noticed Jack shaking his head. 'What's up, Jack?' he asked.

Jack told them, 'Where I live it's very difficult to see the stars because of all the street lights.' He leant over the side of the ship and pointed to lots of areas that appeared lit up far below on the planet's surface where it was presently night-time.

'Sorry to hear that, Jack,' said the Captain. 'I remember that many Earth people, especially in the industrialised parts in the late 20th Century had, through fear, become obsessed with lighting everything up at night which greatly reduced their ability to see the night sky.' Turning to Jack, 'These areas appear to be in places where your people live in very cramped conditions in cities and towns. Even now in your 21st Century there are a few who think everywhere should be artificially lit at night. But more recently many are in favour of reducing this light pollution or removing it all together.'

'It's brilliant up here! I feel so in touch with the wonderful dark sky, full of stars and planets above and around me,' said Jack, 'It would be truly awesome to experience this naturally from the Earth.'

'You can,' said Mas. 'You just need to look for large areas where there are no lights at all. Look Jack, down there.' Jack let out a chuckle as he imagined the reaction of any-one looking up at the night sky from these dark areas and seeing the glow of the ship as it passed steadily and silently above the planet. What might they be imagining…?

Mas helped Jack to recognise some stars and constellations using the chart.

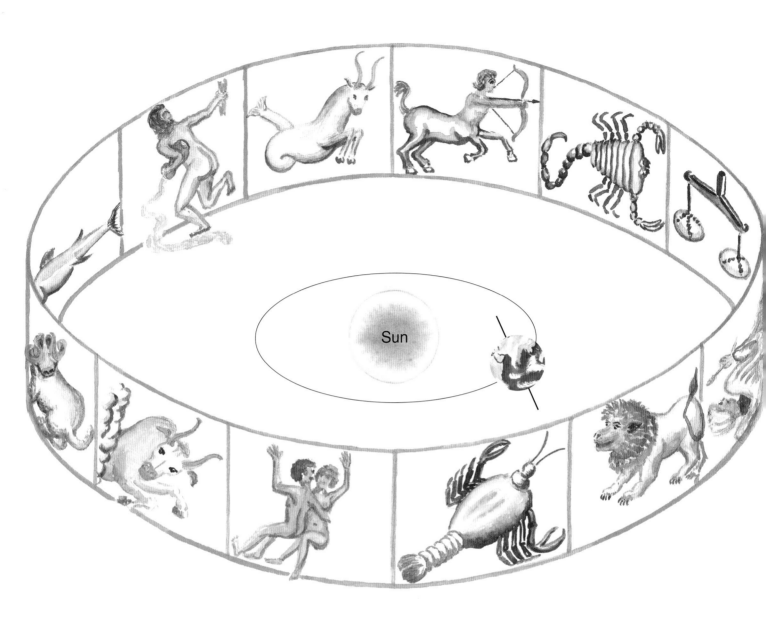

## The Zodiac

The twelve constellations that are on the ecliptic – the background of 'fixed stars' that the Sun and the wanderering stars as they orbit the Sun, appear to travel in front of – as seen from Earth.

This will appear in slightly different places in the night sky depending on the location of the observer on the surface of the Earth and where the Earth is on her orbit round the Sun.

# THE CONSTELLATIONS

Jack was spellbound as Mas explained, 'Your ancestor astronomers on Earth had observed the stars in the night-sky to such a degree that clusters of them appeared to become alive with animal or human form in their imaginations and so they gave names to all these star patterns. Twelve in particular made a ring where the Sun's path or ecliptic appeared to travel. The Greeks named these the Zodiac, taken from the Greek, *zõidiakòs kýklos,* or circle of life figures. It is these animate figures that the Sun appears to pass in front of as viewed from Earth.'

'But what about the scales?' Jack questioned. 'They are man-made, not 'alive'.'
'Originally the Scales of Libra were imagined as being formed from the claws of the Scorpion so they, too, were originally animate.' explained Mas.

| NAME | CONSTELLATION | GLYPH |
|------|--------------|-------|
| Aries | The Ram | ♈ |
| Taurus | The Bull | ♉ |
| Gemini | The Twins | ♊ |
| Cancer | The Crab | ♋ |
| Leo | The Lion | ♌ |
| Virgo | The Virgin | ♍ |
| Libra | The Scales | ♎ |
| Scorpio | The Scorpion | ♏ |
| Sagittarius | The Archer | ♐ |
| Capricornus | The Goat | ♑ |
| Aquarius | The Water Carrier | ♒ |
| Pisces | The Fishes | ♓ |

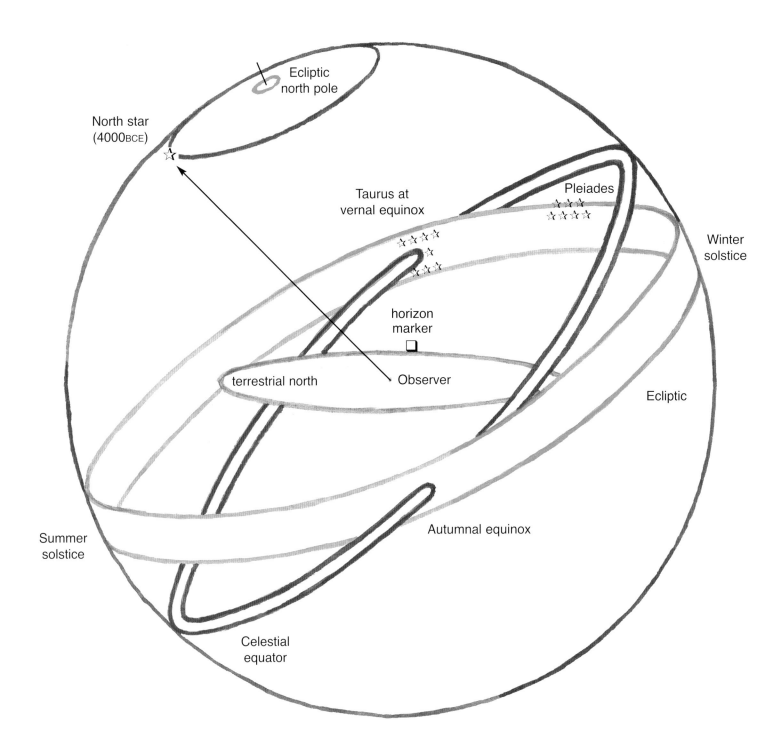

## Precession of the Equinoxes

The Sun's vernal point – this is the point where the Sun's path crosses the celestial equator at the vernal or spring Equinox – is slowly drifting westwards through the twelve zodiac constellations; or we could say the twelve constellations are slipping eastwards.

# THE SIGNIFICANCE OF 2012

The Captain knew it was now time to talk about the reasons for their visit to Earth and so he invited Jack and all the crew to join him. 'I want to take you back in time some 8000 years to an area now known as Mexico and Central America where a culture grew into existence. This culture developed over thousands of years into a very advanced society, known as the Mayans, with a truly remarkable writing system with some 850 symbols known as hieroglyphs which carried meanings that linked the Mayan people, and especially their rulers, to the Cosmos. They devised complicated calendars from their astronomic observations, which was both a daily commitment and a sacred act for the Mayans. Their ability to understand and record the interrelated movements of the Sun, Moon, Earth and Planets, by naked-eye observation over long periods of time, is a clear indication of the sophistication of their society.

A linear calendar, like ours, served their everyday needs, but for everything else their time calculations were based on their belief that time is best measured in cycles, as with the movements of the planets of the solar system. Seventeen of these calendars still exist, all with different functions. But, what made these special was the way they could be interlocked like the cogs of a wheel which then produced the all important 'Long Count' and 'Great Cycle'. The Long Count gave the Mayans a linear view of time that enabled them to record their history, organise their daily routine and plan for the future. They were then able to place these end to end, like building blocks; Great Cycles back into the past and likewise into the future, enabling them to predict planetary alignments and movements with great accuracy.

Unfortunately from 900CE the Mayans declined through famine and disease and were eventually annihilated by invading European cultures in the 15th century. Despite this,

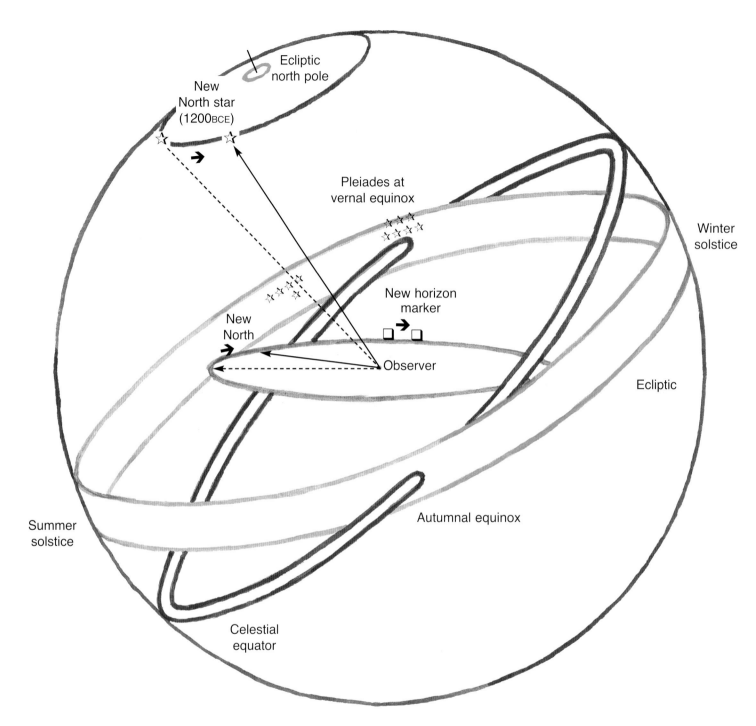

## Precession of the Equinoxes

An observer in the N. Hemisphere in 4000BCE would find that the Sun was rising in Taurus at the vernal equinox. 2,800 years later an observer in the same position would find that Taurus was 'drowning' below the horizon and that the Sun had risen in the Pleiades at vernal equinox; a new marker would need to be placed.

much evidence of their culture remains intact. When the calendars were re-discovered and interpreted in the 20th century, they appeared to end suddenly in the year 2012.'

Jack interrupted, 'Are these the ones that people are saying are a prediction of the end of the planet? Some of my friends and I are scared.'

He was relieved to hear the Captain say, 'Some people thought this interpretation was too simple. They started to research other cultures as well as the Mayans, and began to understand that 2012 marked the end of a Great Cycle, not the end of the Earth.'

The Babylonians and Egyptians had also recorded that, seen from Earth, the Sun appeared to rise each morning in the same zodiac sign for approximately 2,150 years before appearing to progress to rising in the next constellation; this became known as an age. For example, at this present time, some inhabitants of Earth talk of having been in the Piscean age for the last 2000 or more years and are now moving into the age of Aquarius. There being twelve constellations in the zodiac, it followed that it would take some 26,000 years for the Sun to rise through all twelve signs and eventually return to the spot where it had first started, known in some cultures as a 'Great Year'. Indeed, it was found that the Mayans, with their deep understanding of the different cycles of the Sun, Moon, Venus and Mars, had a very accurate method of being able to predict these cycles. Their last recorded Long Count started on the 11th August 3114BCE and, as each comprised 5,126 solar years, is predicted to end on 21st December 2012.

It was this ability to understand what we now know, with the benefit of modern technology, as precession, that was so important: the rotation and imperceptible wobble of the Earth on its axis that changes the location of a constellation, or cluster of stars, over time, when viewed from Earth. The Mayans realised the relationship between this and what they called galactic synchronisation: an event that will bring our solar system into an alignment with a central point in the Milky Way Galaxy, the bright band of stars overhead. The Mayans calculated this Great Cycle to be 25,630 years

# The Mayan Prediction

## Galactic Synchronisation

The Maya calculated this cycle to be 25,630 years based on five 5,126-year world ages.

Other cultures found this cycle to be 25,800 years based on twelve 2,150-year world ages.

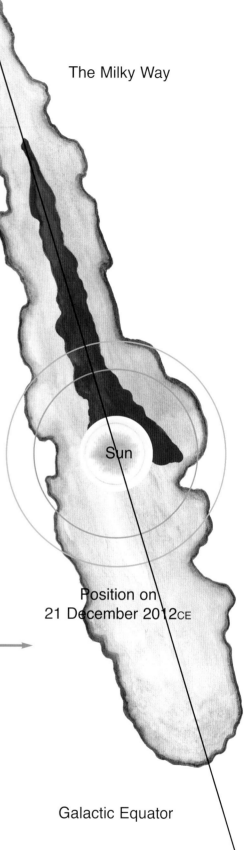

The Milky Way

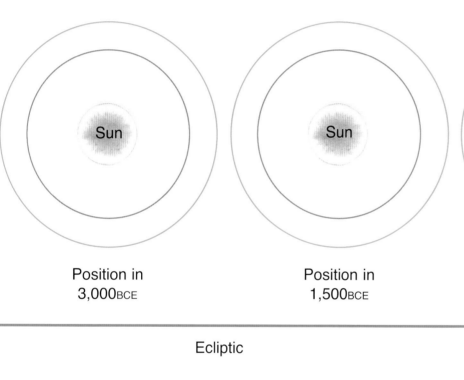

Position in
3,000BCE

Position in
1,500BCE

Position on
21 December 2012CE

Ecliptic

Galactic Equator

based on five Long Counts of 5,126 years each. It follows that the solstice Sun on the 21st December 2012 will align with the equator of our Cosmos, the Milky Way Galaxy, at the galactic core or centre. The Mayan prophecy informs us that this galactic synchronization marks the end of one 'Great Year' and the birth of a new one.'

'Earlier you said approximately 26,000 years, Sir?' asked Mas.

'As I said before, that's because the Earth wobbles as it revolves on its axis. The rotation isn't even, because of the gravitational forces from the Sun, Moon and other planets affecting Earth. This makes accurate calculations difficult, so some accept a 40 year 'window' to accommodate this.'

'So the Sun may already be at the Galactic centre, possibly since 1992, or not until 2032?' enquired Jack.

'There you have it, Jack, but we prefer to think of it as being 2012 because of the accuracy of the Mayan calendars.'

Jack saw the looks on the faces of his friends as they looked at each other with a sense of awe and wonder. 'What are you thinking?' he asked.

Mas responded, 'Just imagine all the observations and recording it must have taken the Mayans and other cultures around the planet to make their predictions. It makes our navigation practice observing with our sextants seem very simple in comparison.'

Jack made a mental note never to complain about his Maths again. He breathed a sigh of relief at all he had just heard; it had answered many of his questions and doubts, although he still found 'precession' not easy to grasp.

'I understand why the old calendars are so important, but why do we need to come to Earth at this time, Sir?' asked Ylime.

'Well, Ylime, that's a very good question. First of all we need to explain all this to as many people on Earth as possible so that they have the choice not to live their lives in fear of some dramatic end to the Earth or indeed to the Cosmos. We might also

IAN THORP 1979

help them to see that they have other choices; things they might wish to change that would seriously benefit humanity as a whole and the planet they inhabit.'

'Do you mean things like pollution and the huge amounts of waste produced each year?' asked Jack, remembering one of his recent lessons at school. 'And the over production of material goods which adds to this?' he added.

'Yes, especially by the industrial societies who have little regard for poorer nations whom they see continue to struggle with food and water supplies,' replied the Captain.

'Surely recycling helps?' interjected Jack. 'We are making an effort at home.'

'Yes, it is a good start.' the Captain replied. 'But it also has to do with how people use their imaginations to bring benefit or harm.'

# THE LAW OF ATTRACTION

'Your friends here, Jack, know that their wishes for good things in their lives have to be balanced with those wishes being extended to include the lives of all others. We on this vessel know of the law of attraction and how that seriously affects our lives. This is only understood by a very few on Earth at this time. Most people believe that outside circumstances affect what comes to them; that other people cause the good or bad things they experience. Others have begun to understand that what happens in their lives is attracted to them by what they hold in their thoughts. So if someone imagines things in a positive way, that is what they will attract to themselves, and conversely if they choose to see things in a negative way then likewise that is what they will attract.'

'So that's why this ship felt so different when I first came on board.' said Jack. 'I have past memories of being on big sailing ships before, but it was always wars and battles with other people being killed and maimed… but this ship is peaceful and has helped me to imagine and experience lots of good things, and not just for me.'

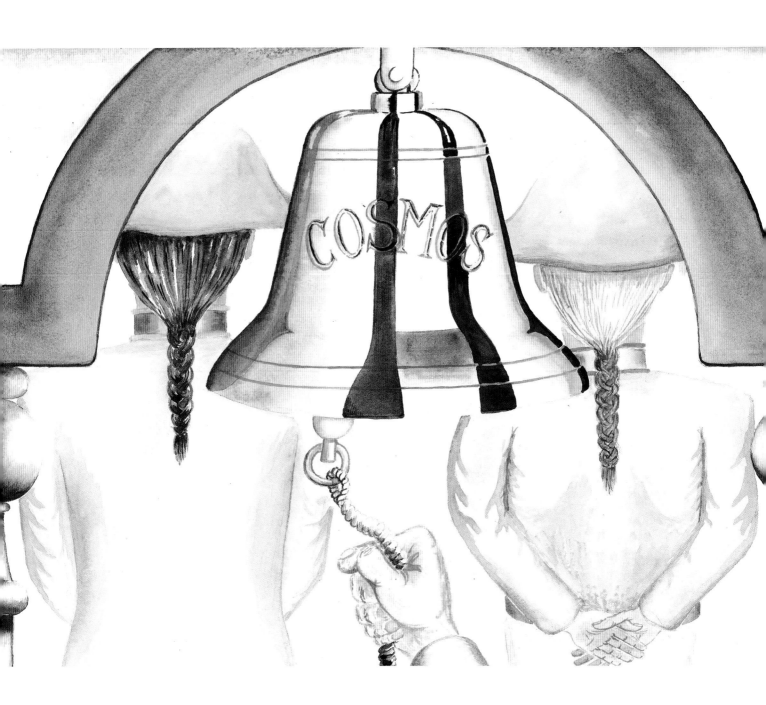

'That's brilliant, Jack,' said Eticilef, 'You have now seen how different thoughts affect what you experience in your life. When you thought that anger and conflict were the way forward that's what you experienced, but since you've been imagining more peaceful ways of doing things, you've found yourself in different surroundings.'

'I want to help this happen' said Jack. 'Imagine if we all stopped blaming other nations, the government, the next-door neighbours or people at school and instead started to imagine positive outcomes we would like to see for everyone's benefit.'

'That would be of great service to your people and the planet, Jack.' added Ylime. They all stood quietly reflecting the deep importance of this to all life.

'We are here to help fan this spark in the people of Earth,' said the Captain, 'especially as many cultures talk of surges of positive energy at special times in the cycles of the Cosmos. Imagine the profound surge that will accompany the beginning of such a significant cycle as 'The Great Year'. If we can enable people to see that the true opportunity here is for a shift in consciousness, they will be encouraged to take personal responsibility for all thoughts and actions in a positive way. This will not only greatly benefit them individually, but the whole of humanity.'

As the ship's company returned to their duties they realised the enormity of the task and each imagined a positive and beneficial passage into the future for their fellow brothers and sisters, the inhabitants of Earth. The Midshipmen showed Jack how to imagine a good outcome so he could join in the exercise with them before sleep.

The Captain went into his private quarters in the stern cabin and quietly thought about the insurge of energy at galactic synchronisation… he imagined it like a series of cog wheels clicking back into place, as if the mechanism of a giant clock was moving round, about to arrive at 12 o'clock and to strike the hour… at that very moment, coinciding with his image, the ship's bell rang out its four double clangs to mark the end of the Forenoon Watch, it being 12 o'clock. He smiled with a degree of satisfaction

at the synchronicity of the moment; as if it confirmed that what he had just imagined may well be a true picture of what was pre-destined to happen.

# THE SOLUTION TO THE TASK

He wished for another synchronicity, otherwise known as 'happenchance' or 'serendipity', to give him the solution to the task.

As he lay back on his 'cot' the Captain started to imagine the different options open to him and his crew in spreading information about the significance of this auspicious time to the inhabitants of the beautiful planet below. So concerned was he for their well-being… …as his thoughts drifted, a picture of a book arose in his imagination. This in turn triggered the memory of all that had been read to him when young… He sprang up and went over to his desk and taking pen and paper from the drawer began to write a story for the children and parents of Earth. He remembered again the lovely myths and legends that had been explained to him by his parents, grandparents and elders. He knew in his heart that this was the most effective way of helping people remember the importance of the times in which they lived and how this would benefit the inhabitants of Earth. Gaia, the ancient Greek name for the goddess of the Earth, would benefit too if they took a greater interest in looking after her needs through more awareness and understanding of where they all lived and their place in the Cosmos.

He had yet to tell the crew of the surprise he had in store for them which was to take them on to the surface of the planet to experience the winter solstice Sun, rising on the shortest day of the year in the Northern Hemisphere. What better than to view it from the very stadium where the Olympic Games had recently been held in London. But this would have to wait until the writing of the book was complete…

When Jack woke up he was surprised to find himself in his own bedroom at home. 'That was some dream!' he thought. 'So real, and with all those deep memories.' Being an inquisitive boy he had often asked for a dream to give him the answers to things he did not understand. He turned on his side and found a book lying on his bedside table. He opened it with a gasp as he recognised Ylime, Mas and Eticilef in one of the pictures and remembered with a mixture of both sadness and excitement, Mas' last words to him for all the children of Earth. *"...remember to go out and find a good dark place in the countryside, away from street lights, where the skies are clear and the stars bright and spend some time looking up to see if you can find Polaris, if you live in the northern hemisphere, or the Southern Cross if you live in the southern hemisphere, and start to identify the constellations of the zodiac and the planets... ...and remember to look out for the glow of the time travellers' ship as it passes high over head..... You never know when we may visit again..."*

Jack also remembered a few references that he had found in the ship's Library. He wrote them down quickly in the back of the book while he still remembered them...

apps GoSkyWatch and astro apps Kairon

Philip's Stargazing Planisphere & Philip's Star Charts Worldwide
from www.octopusbooks.co.uk or local bookshop

and www.heavensabove.com